ABOUT WALT DISNEY ANIMATION STUDIOS ARTIST SHOWCASE BOOKS

This series of original picture books puts the spotlight on the incredible artists of Walt Disney Animation Studios. The pages of each book showcase the personal work of one of these talented artists and introduce a brand-new world and characters.

A special thanks to my husband, Vasil; Katia;
and Benson for their support, help, and encouragement —S. R.

First Hardcover Edition, September 2020

1 3 5 7 9 10 8 6 4 2

FAC-029191-20163

ISBN 978-1-368-02458-7

Printed in Malaysia

This book is set in Halewyn.

Designed by Scott Piehl

Illustrations created with Photoshop

Library of Congress Control Number: 2019952657

Reinforced binding

Visit www.disneybooks.com

Malina's Jam

Concept & illustrations by Svetla Radivoeva

Words by Tammi Sauer

Disney Press

Los Angeles • New York

Malina was a hedgehog who lived in the woods.

She loved her tea. She loved her books.
But most of all, she loved her raspberry garden.

In the spring...

Malina cared for each raspberry bush.

She mulched.

She tugged.

She watered.

"Lovely garden!" called a neighbor squirrel. Malina gave a polite smile.

Later she took a sip of tea, pulled
a book from her bag, and read.
Her raspberry bushes were excellent
listeners.

In the summer...

Malina watched her raspberry garden grow.

And grow.

And grow.

She plucked.

She plopped.

She stirred.

"Nice work!" called a neighbor mouse.

Malina gave a polite smile.

Later she took a sip of tea,
pulled a book from her bag, and read.
Her jars of raspberry jam were excellent listeners, too.

In the fall...

Malina organized her jars
of raspberry jam.

She labeled.

She counted.

She shelved.

"Wow!" called a neighbor rabbit.
"That jam looks amazing."

Malina was so proud she
actually said thank you.

Then she paused.

Maybe she could spare one jar of jam.
"Here," said Malina. "This is for you."

Soon two other neighbors stopped by.
"We heard your raspberry jam is delicious," said a bird.

"Oh," said Malina.
Surely she could part with two more jars.
But before long...

...this happened.

At last, Malina was able to take a sip of tea.
She pulled a book from her bag. Excited to read
to her shelves of jam, she turned and . . . .

"Oh, no!"

Malina hurried to her garden.
She hoped to find enough berries
for one last jar of jam. But
only a single berry was left.

How will I ever make it through
winter with a single raspberry?
Malina wondered as she arrived home.

That's when she heard something.
Lots of somethings.

"Surprise!" shouted her neighbors.

"We wanted to return the favor!" said a rabbit.
"We've brought some jars of goodness for *you!*"
said a mouse.

"Oh! Thanks, everybody!"
said Malina.

Winter came . . .

but as it went, Malina and her neighbors
readied her raspberry garden for the months ahead.

They cleared.

They covered.

They pruned.

Later Malina took a sip of tea,
pulled a book from her bag, and read.
It turned out her neighbors were
excellent listeners, too.

Malina was a hedgehog who lived in the woods.

She loved her tea. She loved her books.
She loved her raspberry garden.
But enjoying these things with her neighbors?

She loved that most of all.

Malina's Jam Recipe

INGREDIENTS

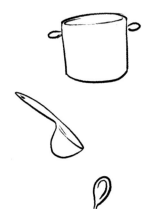

For a neighbor the size of a hedgehog:

70 smashed raspberries (or 2 cups)

4 heaping spoonfuls honey (or 1/4 cup)

4–5 squeezes lemon (or 1 tablespoon)

10 scrapes lemon (or 1 lemon's zest)

For a neighbor the size of a bear (or human):

5 cups smashed raspberries

2 cups honey

2 lemons, juice and zest

DIRECTIONS

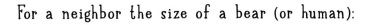

In a large pan, combine raspberries, honey, lemon zest, and lemon juice.

Bring to a boil. Boil for 20 to 30 minutes. Stir regularly until the mixture thickens.

Remove the pan from heat, and funnel jam into sterilized jars.

SHARE WITH NEIGHBORS!

AUTHOR'S NOTE

When I was a little girl living in Bulgaria, I would draw all the time, as well as watch Disney movies. I must have watched *Beauty and the Beast* a thousand times! When I realized that the film, at its core, was made completely of drawings, I was hooked. I decided back then that I wanted to work as an animator.

Fast-forward many years. I took a character animation course at an online school called Animation Mentor, where I had teachers who are professionals in the industry. Once I completed this course, I applied for jobs at animation studios around the world . . .

. . . and I got a job at the Walt Disney Animation Studios. Suddenly, I found myself flying across the Atlantic Ocean to Burbank, California, to become a character animator.

I thought this was my dream come true, and in many ways, it was. But there was so much more to come. At the Walt Disney Animation Studios I'm surrounded by incredibly talented people who know how to push boundaries, and who taught me that being passionate about your work is what it's all about. Working at Disney allows me to grow as an artist every day.

One day, I heard about the Artist Showcase program from a colleague named Benson Shum. His book *Holly's Day at the Pool* was published as part of the program, and he encouraged me to participate. So I did!

I had been wanting to explore an art form different from animation. For *Malina's Jam*, I've had the opportunity to work on the whole project and to take the reader on an emotional journey. When I work as a character animator, I work on little bits and pieces of the whole project. Animation is all about teamwork. Working on a picture book is teamwork, too, but it's a much smaller team. I was also excited to do the illustrations in the book, since drawing has been a constant part of my life. As a computer animator, I don't get to draw as often as I would like.

I remember that, back in Bulgaria, I used to pick raspberries from my grandmother's garden. I was little, and the bushes felt big. My grandmother would take the berries and make them into jam. But I don't think *Malina's Jam* is actually about jam.

The jam is a symbol of Malina's generosity, which is what brings the community together. She has a big heart, but she is also shy. By sharing the jam with other animals, she connects to them without needing to use many words. I know how she feels. I'm shy, too. Luckily, that works just fine when you animate all day long!